T0396782

DEDICATION

To our families who understand why we love to fish. We love you.

Grandpa Phil

Dan, Angela, Reese

Matt, Shantel

Mike, Kaylea, Sutton, Everly

THANK YOU!

ACKNOWLEDGEMENTS

ILLUSTRATOR

Cheryl, whose artistic talents and determination to reach a level of excellence created a book with lasting memories.

EDITOR/WRITING COACH

Jona, whose knowledge of the publishing world was invaluable.

READERS

Hannah, Theresa and Peggy who provided input on changes to the printed word which were used and greatly appreciated.

PHOTOGRAPHER

Scott, who was able to make us look like polished professionals.

PHOTOGRAPHER

Emily, whose skills and expertise captured the spirit of the illustrations.

THE JOHNSON FAMILY…who made this story possible.

TWO BROTHERS & THEIR COUSIN

WRITTEN BY
DEBBIE JOHNSON

ILLUSTRATED BY
CHERYL PAULSON

COPYRIGHT 2023

ALL RIGHTS RESERVED. THIS BOOK OR ANY PORTION THEREOF
MAY NOT BE REPRODUCED OR USED IN ANY MANNER WHATSOEVER
WITHOUT THE EXPRESS WRITTEN PERMISSION OF THE PUBLISHER
EXCEPT FOR THE USE OF BRIEF QUOTATIONS IN A BOOK REVIEW.

ISBN: 979-8-35092-893-8 (PRINT)

Every summer, two brothers, Dakota and Bryce, and their cousin, Grayson, spend a week at THE 80 with Grandpa Phil and Grandma D. THE 80 is a place with a house, a garage and a make-shift whiffle ball field that rests on 80 acres of land along the Clam River in northern Wisconsin. The two brothers and their cousin never know what adventures await them or what is in store for them when they are at THE 80.

Often, during the week, the whole crew ventures off THE 80. But before the adventures begin, the boys help unpack the red truck and put everything where it belongs. When that is done, they start making plans for the week ahead. It is sometimes hard to decide what to do because there are so many choices. One thing is for sure, the ride to Somers Lake in Grandpa's truck is something to look forward to.

Everyone helps pack the truck with fishing supplies, snacks and extra clothes. Then they head south down the curvy gravel road. As Grandpa Phil's truck crests the hill on the dusty road to Somers Lake, the laughter begins and the boys all have smiles on their faces.

Often, during the week, the whole crew ventures off THE 80. But before the adventures begin, the boys help unpack the red truck and put everything where it belongs. When that is done, they start making plans for the week ahead. It is sometimes hard to decide what to do because there are so many choices. One thing is for sure, the ride to Somers Lake in Grandpa's truck is something to look forward to.

Everyone helps pack the truck with fishing supplies, snacks and extra clothes. Then they head south down the curvy gravel road. As Grandpa Phil's truck crests the hill on the dusty road to Somers Lake, the laughter begins and the boys all have smiles on their faces.

They know what is going to happen next. Their arms go up and it feels like they are on a roller coaster ride at the state fair. Each person's stomach is floating and doing a flip at the same time. Excitement is in the air! When they make it to the bottom of the hill, their thoughts turn to Somers Lake, where they will catch sunfish, listen to the croaking frogs and watch the loons gracefully glide along the lake's surface.

After catching some fish at Somers Lake, the group makes their way to Bone Lake. At this lake, there is a park with picnic tables, fire pits, a fishing pier and a dock. Dakota, Grayson and Grandpa Phil head off to the fishing pier while Bryce and Grandma D go to the dock.

Grandma gets out her lawn chair and begins reading a book. She looks up once in a while to check on Bryce. Fish are swimming on all sides of the dock and he lays on his stomach to watch them. Bryce likes to hand fish (this means without a pole). He has gathered some fishing line and tied a hook on the end with a worm as bait to lure in the fish. Suddenly, Grandma hears a big splash and sees that Bryce has fallen into the lake! She runs over to the dock and prepares to scoop him out of the water. Instead, Bryce stands up and looks at Grandma D with the biggest grin on his face – the water was only up to his waist!

Having had enough fishing for the day, the fishing crew heads back to THE 80. They decide they are going to play some whiffle ball before supper. Grandpa Phil is often the pitcher because he throws challenging pitches. You can see the ball swerve and curve as it crosses home plate. Grandma D is an exceptional outfielder and the boys take turns hitting and fielding balls. Ghost runners are often seen on the bases because there are not enough players when the bases are loaded. Sliding, power hitting and great defensive plays are made every time a whiffle ball game is played!

The whiffle ball game ends when Grandma D lets everyone know it is time for supper. Grandma D is strict when it comes to what happens after supper. The boys know once they go inside, there is no going back out. After supper it is shower time, snack time and then into bed to get ready for another day of fishing and adventures. Before the lights turn out, Grandma D reads out loud from some of their treasured books. Each night they choose one book from the collection that was packed. They have discovered they like funny books; ones that give everyone a good belly laugh.

The boys are early risers and wake with the sun. However, the crew is not sure what lake they want to fish at today. Grandpa Phil suggests they make a stop at a local thrift store to check for fishing lures or fishing equipment before deciding the lake of the day. It just so happened that someone dropped off a slew of colorful and unique lures at the thrift store! The two brothers and their cousin each choose a lure carefully. The owner also tells Dakota, Bryce and Grayson a secret… the bass are really biting on Coon Lake. They look at each other with wide eyes. The decision has been made: they are going to fish at Coon Lake!

On their journey to Coon Lake, the boys talk about the best fishing bait for bass. They conclude that frogs might be at the top of the list. While Dakota, Grayson and Grandpa Phil take the trail to fish from shore, Grandma D and Bryce walk further along the trail and go to the back waters of Coon Lake to hunt for frogs. They can hear the frogs croaking as they move slowly and silently through the swampy, muddy backwaters. Bryce knows that frog hunting can be tricky, especially when he steps and gradually sinks into the mud that goes halfway up his boots. Grandma D hangs onto Bryce's left hand tightly as he reaches for the frogs with his right. After catching enough frogs for the day, Grandma D and Bryce take the trail back to where the others are already fishing.

Dakota and Grayson are really excited to see all the frogs Bryce has caught. They each take a frog, use it as bait and wait to see what happens. Sure enough, the frogs turn out to be just the right bait and Dakota catches a huge bass! Dakota is a skilled fisherman and sometimes Grayson and Bryce ask him to help with tangled lines and baiting hooks. The boys spend the day fishing at Coon Lake and talk about the man who told them where the bass were biting. Many fish are caught and pictures are taken to capture the memories. After another day of fishing, it is back to THE 80 for whiffle ball and evening stories.

The next day, the adventures continue and it is on to Little Butternut Lake. Grandpa rented a pontoon boat for the day and the entire crew helps the Boat Man unload the boat at the dock. Everyone climbs aboard, puts on their life jackets and they motor away for a day of fishing with Grandpa Phil at the helm. The fishing was not the greatest, so they kept moving to different spots. Even though the boys did not realize it, Grandpa Phil and Grandma D always had their eyes on the sky.

The blue sky started to turn an ominous color of gray as dark clouds rolled in. The two brothers and their cousin could see Grandpa Phil was getting nervous. They headed closer to the boat landing and Grandma D called the Boat Man. The clouds in the sky thickened and the wind began to blow. Soon the boat began to sway from side to side. Everyone knew they needed to get onto dry land quickly. Grandpa Phil steered the boat to the landing and saw the Boat Man ready and waiting for them. Dakota, Bryce and Grayson thought a new record was set for the fastest time a boat had ever been taken out of a lake and loaded onto a boat trailer. After loading the boat, the whole crew ran to Grandpa Phil's red truck and waited out the thunderstorm!

After the close call on Little Butternut Lake, Grayson, Dakota and Bryce wanted to go back to THE 80 and try their skills at designing and constructing some new fishing lures. Grandma D had bought the supplies before leaving for The 80. All they needed to make the lures were hooks, feathers, colored duct tape and aluminum squares cut from pop cans. Grandpa Phil showed them a basic lure design from a fishing magazine. From that design, the boys took their time and each made a unique and colorful fishing lure. They ended up with a new lure for their tackle boxes!

There was still time left in the day and another adventure to be had! Dakota, Bryce and Grayson like taking four-wheeler rides. The fishing rods and tackle boxes are put into the back of the four-wheeler for the trip. THE 80 has many trails, game cameras and food plots for deer. There's a variety of animal markings, giving clues about what kinds of animals call THE 80 home. They know it is going to be a bumpy ride because pocket gophers have dug holes along the trail. While on the ride, they gather up the game camera memory cards and drive down to the Clam River for some fishing. As they get closer to the river, Grandpa Phil reminds everyone to hold back the branches so that no one gets one in their eye. They spend some time fishing on the Clam River, finding the deep holes with fish, and then head back to the house to finish the day. At the end of the day, they look at the game camera memory cards on Grandpa Phil's computer and the boys see deer, bear, fox and other wildlife.

So far this week, all the fishing has taken place close to THE 80. Grandpa Phil decides a new adventure awaits on the St. Croix River, where they would again try their luck at bass fishing. The two brothers and their cousin caught some fish, but what they really wondered about was what was under a nearby bridge. The boys began exploring and saw there was a small creek that flowed into the St. Croix River. In the creek were large boulders and rocks. The threesome knew there were treasures underneath those rocks.

Slowly, carefully and attentively, they turn over the rocks and discover all sizes of crayfish! The boys knew they needed to keep some because crayfish work well for bait. The boys yell for Grandma D to find containers for their great discovery. She dashes off to the red truck to find something to put them in. The crayfish catching lasted for hours! Finally, Grandpa Phil let the boys know it was time to head back to THE 80. The boys climbed up the creek bank, sat in a circle and went through their collection and only kept the best crayfish for future fishing adventures.

Another favorite activity for the week was hunting for snakes and turtles. Bryce is an expert at catching snakes. He watches where they go into the grass and he waits at that spot without making a sound. Sooner or later, the snake comes back out in the same spot. Bryce snatches the snake and holds it, waiting for Grayson and Dakota to come over and take a look. They are impressed with how fast Bryce can catch a snake! Grayson prefers catching turtles and he often finds them on shore or at the end of his fishing line. The turtles he catches are colorful with very hard shells. Once everyone has seen the turtles, he puts them back into their natural habitat. The snakes, turtles and fish caught during the stay at THE 80 are part of what Grandpa Phil calls "The Catch and Release Program."

Before the week at THE 80 ends, Dakota, Bryce and Grayson insist on a visit to Clear Lake. They arrive at the perfect time. There are no crowds, bright sunshine and crystal-clear water. It is the perfect lake to swim and fish in at the same time. Swimsuits, goggles, fishing poles, tackle boxes, green worms and nightcrawlers are important supplies for this adventure. There is a swimming beach and off to the west is a patch of weeds in the lake. The boys wonder what is lurking in the weeds, so they toss their fishing lines in and come out with a small sunfish and a bass. While swimming, they use the goggles to search for treasures at the bottom of the swimming beach. They each come up with different treasures… colorful rocks, coins, a fishing lure and a ring.

It is the final day of fishing for the week. Grandpa Phil gives the okay to take his fishing boat to Big Doctor Lake. This lake is where the two brothers and their cousin hope to catch some big Northern Pike. As they are trolling along the lake, Dakota feels a big fish on his line. He uses all his strength to reel it in. He knows he is going to need help landing the fish in the boat, so Bryce grabs the net. Just before the boys catch the fish in the net, Dakota's line snaps! They watch the big Northern swim away. Disappointed but not defeated, they keep on fishing and end up with some fantastic fish stories to share with family and friends.

The week at THE 80 is coming to an end, so Dakota, Bryce and Grayson play their last game of whiffle ball, take a four-wheeler ride to the Clam River and organize their tackle boxes. They follow the nightly routine and, on the final day, help pack Grandpa Phil's red truck. They head down the gravel driveway toward home. The boys talk about the week's highlights and if they will be able to have a week at THE 80 again next year. Grandpa Phil and Grandma D reassure them it will happen. The two brothers and their cousin start thinking about the adventures awaiting them and wonder what is going to happen next summer.

Debbie Johnson, also known as Grandma D, is from South Dakota and is a retired educator who worked as a teacher, principal and superintendent. She now works at her community library and drives a school bus. Debbie has been married to her husband, Phil, for 40 years and is the mother of three and a grandmother of six. She has been thinking about writing a children's book for over 20 years; her three oldest grandsons inspired her to write *Three Brothers and Their Cousin*.

Bryce, Dakota and Grayson are Debbie's three oldest grandsons. Their summers are spent fishing, swimming, playing baseball and football. They have special memories of THE 80 and helped Grandma D write the story of *Two Brothers and Their Cousin*. Grayson lives in South Dakota; Dakota and Bryce live in Wisconsin.

Cheryl Paulson is a retired art teacher who now has a pottery studio and artist's workspace in her home. The heart of her teaching career was at the Crow Creek Tribal School. She lives with her husband, Glen, on a bluff above the Missouri River, where she gathers inspiration for her pottery work, drawings and paintings. This is her first illustrated book.